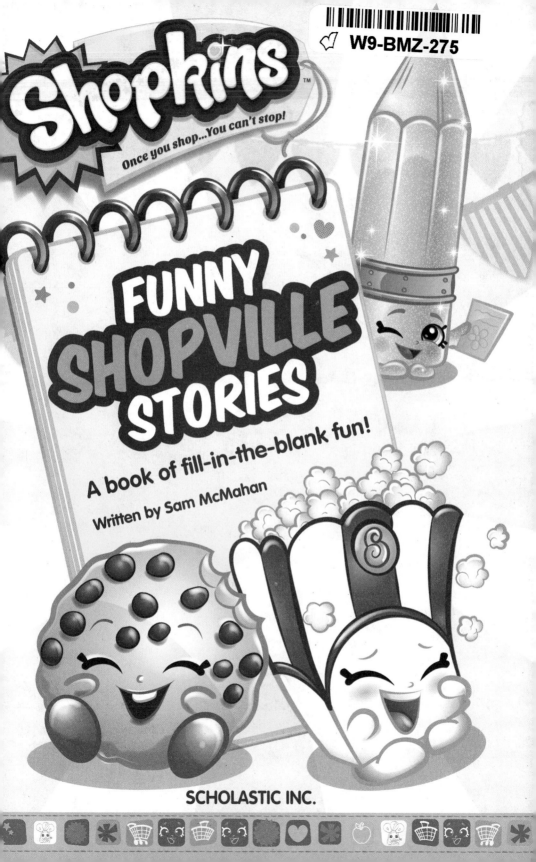

# Shopkins™

Once you shop...You can't stop!

# FUNNY SHOPVILLE STORIES

### A book of fill-in-the-blank fun!

Written by Sam McMahan

SCHOLASTIC INC.

Published by Scholastic Inc., *Publishers since 1920.* SCHOLASTIC and associated logos are trademarks and/or registered trademarks of Scholastic Inc.

The publisher does not have any control over and does not assume any responsibility for author or third-party websites or their content.

This book is a work of fiction. Names, characters, places, and incidents are either the product of the author's imagination or are used fictitiously, and any resemblance to actual persons, living or dead, business establishments, events, or locales is entirely coincidental.

ISBN 978-0-545-92556-3

12 11 10 9 8 7 6 5 4 3 2 1          15 16 17 18 19 20

Printed in the U.S.A.          40
First printing, 2015

# WELCOME TO SMALL MART!

The Shopkins™ who live here have cartloads of shopping fun every day. There are so many adventures in store for Apple Blossom, Sneaky Sally, Toasty Pop, and all their friends—including you! To join in the fun, try finishing these fill-in stories. They can be played with a friend or a group or even by yourself.

## HOW DO YOU PLAY?

Just grab a pen and get ready to make up words to fill in the blanks in each story. Players will need to think of nouns, verbs, adjectives, food items, animals, colors, places, and more.

**IT'S AS SIMPLE AS 1-2-3!**

**1.** Pick a story from this book—but don't read it ahead of time!

**2.** Ask the other players for words to fill in the blanks on the page before the story.

**3.** Read the completed story and enjoy the hilarious Shopkins adventure—written by you!

## BIG LAUGHS ARE IN THE BAG WITH THESE FUNNY SHOPKINS STORIES. ONCE YOU SHOP, YOU CAN'T STOP!

# WELCOME TO SMALL MART!

PLURAL NOUN _____

VERB _____

FUNNY WORD _____

VERB ENDING IN —ING _____

PIECE OF CLOTHING _____

ADJECTIVE _____

PLURAL NOUN _____

PLURAL NOUN _____

NOUN _____

PART OF THE BODY _____

ADJECTIVE _____

VERB ENDING IN —ING _____

VERB _____

Have you ever dreamed of visiting a world inhabited by

friendly little _____ who love to shop till they
PLURAL NOUN

_____? If your answer is "_____," then slip on
VERB                                           FUNNY WORD

your _____ _____ and get ready to explore
VERB ENDING IN —ING     PIECE OF CLOTHING

Small Mart, where shopping fun is in the bag. The Fruit and

Veg aisle is jam-packed with _____ Shopkins who
ADJECTIVE

are bursting with personality, good taste, and _____.
PLURAL NOUN

"Well-bread" Shopkins who savor the finer _____ in
PLURAL NOUN

life are found in the Bakery aisle. The Shopkins from the Party

Foods aisle are always ready to celebrate at the drop of a/an

_____. The Shopkins in the Cleaning and Laundry
NOUN

aisle are eager to lend a helping _____ to keep
PART OF THE BODY

everything looking tidy and smelling _____. And
ADJECTIVE

the Shopkins in the Shoe and Fashion aisle will have you

_____ your very best. Once you've visited Small
VERB ENDING IN —ING

Mart, you won't ever want to _____! Check you later!
VERB

# GET YOUR FOOT IN THE GAME

VERB ENDING IN -ING _____

NOUN _____

VERB ENDING IN -ING _____

ADJECTIVE _____

NOUN _____

ADJECTIVE _____

PLURAL NOUN _____

NOUN _____

PLURAL NOUN _____

NOUN _____

ADJECTIVE _____

ADJECTIVE _____

Sneaky Wedge always looks forward to _____ in

*VERB ENDING IN —ING*

the annual Shopville Games. She wins a gold _____

*NOUN*

every year! How does she get herself in such great

_____ shape each year? She takes it one

*VERB ENDING IN —ING*

_____ step at a time! The sole focus of this

*ADJECTIVE*

footloose and fancy-free _____ is to get into tip-top

*NOUN*

condition well before the games begin. She kicks off her daily

_____ workout by flexing her _____ and

*ADJECTIVE*                                              *PLURAL NOUN*

running laps around the _____. She builds strength

*NOUN*

and endurance by climbing up and down shelves of

_____ in the Homewares aisle. She improves

*PLURAL NOUN*

her balance by carefully standing on piles of fresh

_____-melons in the Fruit and Veg aisle. When it

*NOUN*

comes to just doing her best, Sneaky Wedge puts her

_____ foot down. She wants to win! Her motto is

*ADJECTIVE*

"Go _____ or go home!"

*ADJECTIVE*

# BUTTERING UP HER FRIEND

ADJECTIVE _____

NOUN _____

NOUN _____

A PLACE _____

ADJECTIVE _____

PLURAL NOUN _____

ADJECTIVE _____

PLURAL NOUN _____

PART OF THE BODY _____

ADJECTIVE _____

NOUN _____

PART OF THE BODY _____

Toasty Pop is known for popping up at random to give

_____ toasts. Let's listen in as this warmhearted
ADJECTIVE

_____ praises her favorite _____ in all of
NOUN                                          NOUN

(the) _____ , Margarine:
A PLACE

Margarine, you've been there for me ever since

I was a little, _____ loaf. You spread happiness,
ADJECTIVE

laughter, and _____ wherever you go—that's
PLURAL NOUN

just how you roll. Whenever I yeast expect it, I'm

reminded of how _____ we are to have each
ADJECTIVE

other as best _____, and I smile from
PLURAL NOUN

ear to _____! No matter how you slice it, hanging
PART OF THE BODY

out with you is always a/an _____ adventure.
ADJECTIVE

Our friendship will never grow stale. I knead you in my

life, and I crust you completely. You make me

want to be a butter _____—and I love you
NOUN

with all my _____ !
PART OF THE BODY

# MOVIE TIME
## WITH
## POPPY CORN

VERB _____

ADJECTIVE _____

ADJECTIVE _____

PLURAL NOUN _____

FRIEND'S NAME _____

FAMOUS PERSON _____

VERB ENDING IN –ING _____

NOUN _____

ADJECTIVE _____

FRIEND (MALE) _____

COLOR _____

NOUN _____

A PLACE _____

PLURAL NOUN _____

VERB ENDING IN –ING _____

*Poppy Corn loves to sit back, _____, and enjoy a/an*
VERB

_____ *movie, especially classic Shopkins flicks like:*
ADJECTIVE

● MARY SHOPPINS— **A magically _____ nanny is**

**hired to mind a pair of mischievous _____**
PLURAL NOUN

**named _____ and _____. She teaches**
FRIEND'S NAME          FAMOUS PERSON

**them how to shop while singing, dancing, and _____.**
VERB ENDING IN —ING

● SHOPPING BEAUTY— **A beautiful princess, cursed by a**

**wicked _____ , falls into a deep, _____**
NOUN                          ADJECTIVE

**sleep after an exhausting shopping spree. She can only be**

**awakened by a kiss from her true love, Prince _____.**
FRIEND (MALE)

● CARTS— **A bright _____ race cart named Speedy**
COLOR

**Mc_____ is trying to get to the championship**
NOUN

**race in (the) _____ but ends up in a run-down store**
A PLACE

**instead. Speedy becomes friends with the town's resident**

**_____ and ultimately learns that _____**
PLURAL NOUN                    VERB ENDING IN —ING

**isn't everything.**

# SHOP, MOP, AND ROLL

ANIMAL _____

ADJECTIVE _____

ADVERB _____

VERB _____

NOUN _____

PLURAL NOUN _____

VERB ENDING IN –ING _____

TYPE OF LIQUID _____

ADJECTIVE _____

VERB _____

NOUN _____

ADJECTIVE _____

Molly Mops is as busy as a/an _____ , spending
ANIMAL

most of her time doing _____ chores around Small
ADJECTIVE

Mart while singing that _____ popular working
ADVERB

tune, "Whistle While You _____." But this
VERB

hardworking little _____ knows how to clean up
NOUN

at having fun, too! When she's not scrubbing the tiled

_____ or getting a handle on anything that needs
PLURAL NOUN

wiping, polishing, or _____ , Molly loves to play
VERB ENDING IN —ING

mopscotch. Molly likes to help others have fun, too.

Sometimes she'll leave a trail of _____ on the floor
TYPE OF LIQUID

so Betty Boot and her _____ sole mates can skate,
ADJECTIVE

slide, and _____. Dum Mee Mee and the other
VERB

babies love when she makes _____-shaped
NOUN

bubbles for them to chase. Molly Mops knows how to wring

every last drop of fun out of a busy, _____ day.
ADJECTIVE

# ORANGE YOU GLAD SHE CAN KEEP A SECRET?

ADJECTIVE _____

PLURAL NOUN _____

VERB ENDING IN -ING _____

ADJECTIVE _____

ADJECTIVE _____

FAMOUS PERSON _____

NOUN _____

VERB _____

FOOD ITEM (PLURAL) _____

PART OF THE BODY (PLURAL) _____

ADJECTIVE _____

ADJECTIVE _____

Juicy Orange liked to learn _____ secrets about

*ADJECTIVE*

her friends. Most of the time, her friends loved telling her

their pulpy _____, but sometimes she had to squeeze

*PLURAL NOUN*

the secrets out of them. And once in a while, if she was

_____ in the right place at the _____ time

*VERB ENDING IN —ING*                                      *ADJECTIVE*

in Small Mart, she overheard the most _____ secrets

*ADJECTIVE*

of all. For example, Juicy Orange learned that Cupcake Chic

would chant, "I am the Future Mrs. _____"

*FAMOUS PERSON*

in her sleep. She also discovered that little Dum Mee Mee was

so frightened of the boogey_____ that the mere

*NOUN*

mention of the word would make her _____ like a

*VERB*

baby. And that Poppy Corn was always causing avalanches of

_____—she is quite a butter_____.

*FOOD ITEM  (PLURAL)*                          *PART OF THE BODY (PLURAL)*

Secrets held a lot of a-peel for Juicy Orange. Luckily, she was a

sweet, _____ fruit, and everyone knew their secrets

*ADJECTIVE*

were _____ with her.

*ADJECTIVE*

# SNEAKY SALLY STEPS OUT

NOUN _____

ADJECTIVE _____

NOUN _____

ADJECTIVE _____

NOUN _____

A PLACE _____

VEGETABLE (PLURAL) _____

FUNNY WORD _____

PLURAL NOUN _____

ADJECTIVE _____

FRIEND'S NAME _____

VERB _____

PART OF THE BODY (PLURAL) _____

VERB _____

Sneaky Sally was excited when Prommy, a friendly, high-heeled _____ , invited her to go out for a/an
<sub>NOUN</sub>

_____ night on the town. Sally wasn't a fancy
<sub>ADJECTIVE</sub>

_____ and didn't know what to expect. When
<sub>NOUN</sub>

the _____ friends left Small Mart, they were
<sub>ADJECTIVE</sub>

picked up in a chauffeured _____ and driven all
<sub>NOUN</sub>

the way to (the) _____. Prommy told Sally they
<sub>A PLACE</sub>

were going to see the _____ in concert, and
<sub>VEGETABLE (PLURAL)</sub>

Sally squealed, "_____!" The girls had front-row
<sub>FUNNY WORD</sub>

_____, and Sally spent the night shaking her
<sub>PLURAL NOUN</sub>

_____ laces in time to the music. The band's
<sub>ADJECTIVE</sub>

lead singer, _____, even pulled Sally up on stage
<sub>FRIEND'S NAME</sub>

to _____ with the band. She had a smile from ear
<sub>VERB</sub>

to _____! *I'll remember this night for as long*
<sub>PART OF THE BODY (PLURAL)</sub>

*as I* _____*! she thought.*
<sub>VERB</sub>

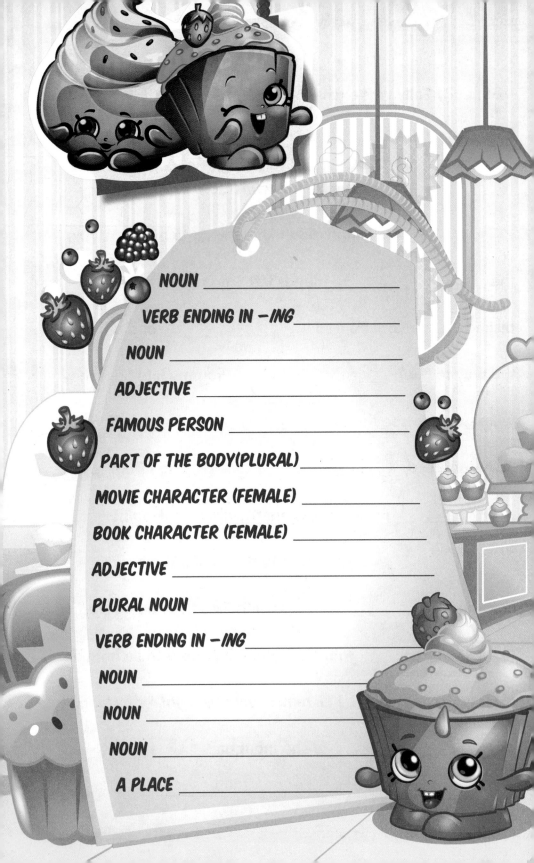

NOUN _____

VERB ENDING IN –ING _____

NOUN _____

ADJECTIVE _____

FAMOUS PERSON _____

PART OF THE BODY(PLURAL) _____

MOVIE CHARACTER (FEMALE) _____

BOOK CHARACTER (FEMALE) _____

ADJECTIVE _____

PLURAL NOUN _____

VERB ENDING IN –ING _____

NOUN _____

NOUN _____

NOUN _____

A PLACE _____

Cupcake Chic was one glamorous _____. She

NOUN

enjoyed posing, _____ , and strutting her sweet

VERB ENDING IN —ING

stuff for every _____ to see. In fact, this fashionably

NOUN

_____ treat was considered the _____

ADJECTIVE                                                    FAMOUS PERSON

of the Bakery aisle. She wasn't just another pretty

_____ , though. She was a talented actress,

PART OF THE BODY (PLURAL)

perfect for roles like _____ or even

MOVIE CHARACTER (FEMALE)

_____. On days when Cupcake Chic

BOOK CHARACTER (FEMALE)

really wanted to show off her _____ fashion

ADJECTIVE

sense, she added some extra frosting to her top, making this

stylish Shopkin look like a million _____! She

PLURAL NOUN

dreamed of someday _____ on the cover of a

VERB ENDING IN —ING

famous fashion _____—or, better yet, on a

NOUN

giant, flashing _____ in the middle of Times

NOUN

Square! *Lights, camera,* _____! Look out,

NOUN

(the) _____—here comes Cupcake Chic!

A PLACE

# SHOPKINS SPREE

VERB ENDING IN –ING _____

PLURAL NOUN _____

ADJECTIVE _____

VERB (PAST TENSE) _____

PART OF THE BODY (PLURAL) _____

PLURAL NOUN _____

NOUN _____

ANIMAL _____

PLURAL NOUN _____

ADJECTIVE _____

ADVERB _____

PLURAL NOUN _____

TYPE OF LIQUID _____

**This is Ace Reporter, live from Small Mart, where**

**Team Spilt Milk just set a new record for** _____ **in the**

VERB ENDING IN —ING

**"Cleanup in Aisle 7 Dash."**

**Ace:** Explain to the _____ watching at home

PLURAL NOUN

how this _____ event works.

ADJECTIVE

**Spilt:** Well, I _____ in a shopping basket while

VERB (PAST TENSE)

Cheeky Chocolate pushed me as fast as her little

_____ would go! My job was to fill the

PART OF THE BODY (PLURAL)

basket with _____ before we got to the

PLURAL NOUN

end of the aisle. I stockpiled everything from a juicy,

_____ to _____-shaped

NOUN                                    ANIMAL

_____ to _____ toilet paper.

PLURAL NOUN                          ADJECTIVE

**Ace:** It was a/an _____ scary moment when

ADVERB

your basket toppled over, but you were so brave!

I would've burst into _____.

PLURAL NOUN

**Spilt:** Ace, you know what they say—there's no use crying

over spilt _____.

TYPE OF LIQUID

ADJECTIVE _____

ADJECTIVE _____

PART OF THE BODY (PLURAL) _____

NOUN _____

PIECE OF CLOTHING _____

NUMBER _____

PLURAL NOUN _____

ADJECTIVE _____

PART OF THE BODY (PLURAL) _____

NOUN _____

PLURAL NOUN _____

FUNNY WORD _____

FAMOUS PERSON _____

VERB _____

ADJECTIVE _____

ANIMAL _____

When shy, _____ Kooky Cookie won the title *Miss*
                ADJECTIVE

_____ *Shopville*, the other Shopkins couldn't believe
  ADJECTIVE

their _____! Kooky offered this advice on how
        PART OF THE BODY (PLURAL)

to become a beauty pageant _____:
                                    NOUN

● Instead of wearing a designer _____ that costs
                                      PIECE OF CLOTHING

_____ _____ to make, try making a/an
    NUMBER            PLURAL NOUN

_____ outfit with your own two _____.
   ADJECTIVE                              PART OF THE BODY (PLURAL)

● If you are asked a question like, "If you had one wish in the

world, what would it be?" say something about making

the _____ a better place for all the other
          NOUN

_____ to live in—or just say "_____."
   PLURAL NOUN                            FUNNY WORD

Whatever you do, do not say how much you'd like to meet

_____.
  FAMOUS PERSON

● Finally, winning is all about presentation. So when you

_____ in front of the _____ judges,
      VERB                              ADJECTIVE

make sure to glide with the grace of a/an _____.
                                              ANIMAL

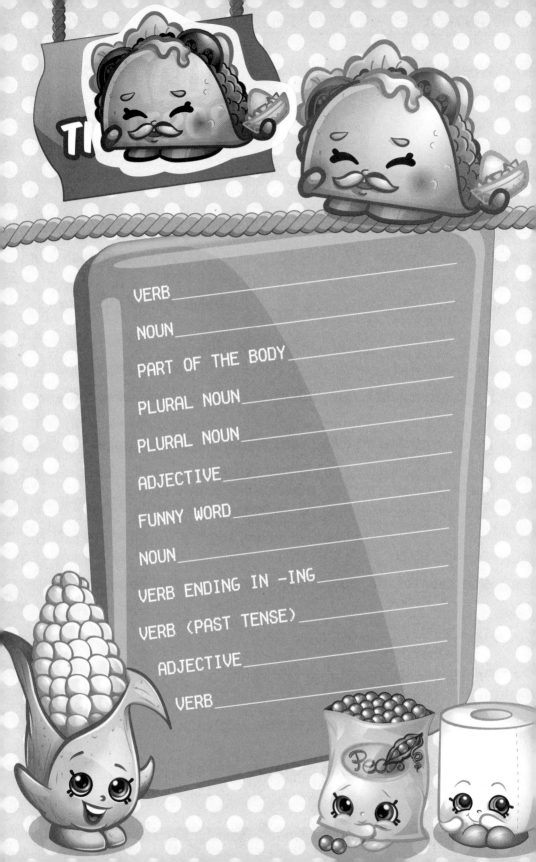

VERB_____

NOUN_____

PART OF THE BODY_____

PLURAL NOUN_____

PLURAL NOUN_____

ADJECTIVE_____

FUNNY WORD_____

NOUN_____

VERB ENDING IN -ING_____

VERB (PAST TENSE)_____

ADJECTIVE_____

VERB_____

Taco Terrie was going to attempt the first-ever tightrope

_____ across Aisle 1. A crowd of Shopkins
VERB

gathered as he carefully placed one _____ on the
NOUN

rope, then the other. Step by step, inch by inch, he moved

across. When he got to the middle, his _____
PART OF THE BODY

suddenly slipped. Bits of chopped _____ and
PLURAL NOUN

shredded _____ spilled from his shell toward the
PLURAL NOUN

ground and landed on the _____ spectators.
ADJECTIVE

"_____!" Terrie cried in Spanish. He paused for a
FUNNY WORD

moment before continuing, fearing that the thumping of his

_____ would knock him off balance again. Soon
NOUN

he was slowly _____ along on the tightrope.
VERB ENDING IN —ING

The Shopkins _____ loudly when he was
VERB (PAST TENSE)

safely on the other side. Taco Terrie took a/an _____
ADJECTIVE

bow and said, "You never know what you can do until you

_____!"
VERB

# SUNDAE'S WEATHER FORECAST

NOUN_____

ADJECTIVE_____

PLURAL NOUN_____

NOUN_____

NUMBER_____

NOUN_____

ADJECTIVE_____

PLURAL NOUN_____

NOUN_____

NOUN_____

TYPE OF LIQUID_____

PLURAL NOUN_____

ADJECTIVE_____

PLURAL NOUN_____

PLURAL NOUN_____

**Good day, Shopkins! This is Suzie Sundae with the**

_____ **forecast. Today in Frozen Foods, it's**
   NOUN

**supposed to be** _____ **with a chance of**
                        ADJECTIVE

_____ **. With** _____ **gusts, temperatures**
   PLURAL NOUN                   NOUN

**will plummet to** _____ **below zero—perfect for a**
                        NUMBER

**freezer-loving** _____ **like me! Those who aren't**
                        NOUN

**accustomed to extreme,** _____ **temperatures are**
                                ADJECTIVE

**warned to keep their** _____ **covered with a warm**
                             PLURAL NOUN

_____ **to avoid frostbite. Over in the Fruit and**
   NOUN

**Veg aisle of Small Mart, Shopkins can expect** _____
                                                        NOUN

**showers this afternoon. Sprinkles of** _____ **will fall**
                                            TYPE OF LIQUID

**every hour on the leafy green** _____ **. And the lucky**
                                      PLURAL NOUN

**Shopkins in the Bakery aisle can look forward to warm,**

_____ **temperatures with a light breeze blowing in**
   ADJECTIVE

**the scent of sugar, cinnamon, and spicy** _____
                                                  PLURAL NOUN

**from the direction of the Pantry. Rain or** _____ **,**
                                                  PLURAL NOUN

**I hope you enjoy your day!**

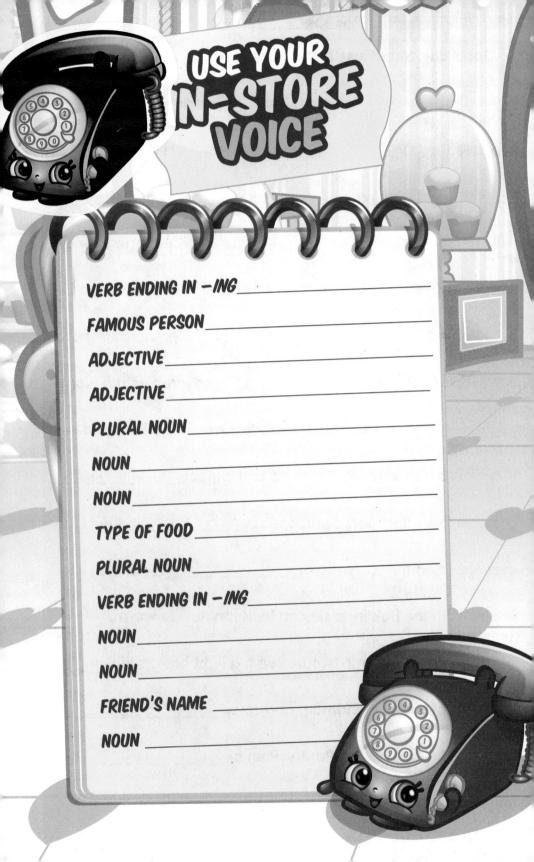

# USE YOUR IN-STORE VOICE

VERB ENDING IN —ING _____

FAMOUS PERSON _____

ADJECTIVE _____

ADJECTIVE _____

PLURAL NOUN _____

NOUN _____

NOUN _____

TYPE OF FOOD _____

PLURAL NOUN _____

VERB ENDING IN —ING _____

NOUN _____

NOUN _____

FRIEND'S NAME _____

NOUN _____

The Shopkins would burst out _____
<br>*VERB ENDING IN —ING*

hysterically whenever Chatter used his _____
<br>*FAMOUS PERSON*

impression to deliver funny, _____ in-store
<br>*ADJECTIVE*

announcements like these:

◉ Check out today's special in the _____
<br>*ADJECTIVE*

   Fruit and Veg aisle—buy a bag of Granny Smith

   _____ , get a fresh, _____ free!
<br>*PLURAL NOUN*       *NOUN*

◉ Shoppers, stop by the Bakery aisle to see our newest

   selection of _____-shaped, _____
<br>*NOUN*       *TYPE OF FOOD*

   -flavored layer cakes made with premium _____.
<br>*PLURAL NOUN*

◉ Parents, please remind your children there's no

   _____ in the store unless accompanied by
<br>*VERB ENDING IN —ING*

   a/an _____.
<br>*NOUN*

◉ For the customer who wanted the six-foot-tall stuffed

   _____ nicknamed "_____
<br>*NOUN*       *FRIEND'S NAME*

   Fluffypants," a sales associate will help you load it onto

   your _____.
<br>*NOUN*

NOUN _____

NUMBER _____

  PLURAL NOUN _____

    ADJECTIVE _____

      VERB _____

        FAVORITE SHOPKIN _____

          NOUN _____

VERB (PAST TENSE) _____

ADJECTIVE _____

NOUN _____

VERB ENDING IN -ING _____

ADJECTIVE _____

FUNNY WORD _____

NOUN _____

NOUN BEGINNING WITH P _____

It was the final _____ball game of the season.
NOUN

Team Hat was losing to Team Fruit and Veg by _____
NUMBER

_____. The Hats were down to their last
PLURAL NOUN

_____ batter. Casper Cap stepped up to the plate
ADJECTIVE

to _____, brimming with excitement. "C'mon,
VERB

Casper!" shouted Coach _____. The pitcher,
FAVORITE SHOPKIN

Juicy Orange, spat out a seed and hurled a pitch over the

_____. Casper swung and _____.
NOUN                                         VERB (PAST TENSE)

*Strike one!* The next pitch was _____ and
ADJECTIVE

just a bit outside. Ball one! Juicy Orange then fired a/an

_____ right down the middle, and Casper
NOUN

smashed it. Peachy began _____ backward to
VERB ENDING IN —ING

catch it, but it was going . . . going . . . _____!
ADJECTIVE

It landed with a/an "_____" in the Bakery aisle,
FUNNY WORD

and the _____ went wild! Casper was crowned
NOUN

MVP—Most Valuable _____.
NOUN BEGINNING WITH P